MINIONS

Who's the Boss?

MINIONS MOVIE: WHO'S THE BOSS?
A CENTUM BOOK 9781910114865

Published in Great Britain by Centum Books Ltd

This edition published 2015
2015 © Universal Studios Licensing LLC.

1 3 5 7 9 10 8 6 4 2

Centum Books Ltd, Unit 1, Upside Station Building, Solsbro Road,
Torquay, Devon, UK, TQ2 6FD

books@centumbooksltd.co.uk

CENTUM BOOKS Limited Reg. No. 07641486

A CIP catalogue record for this book is available from the British
Library

Printed in Slovakia

MINIONS
Who's the Boss?

by Lucy Rosen

centum

Attention, Minions fans!
Look for these words when you read
this book. Can you spot them all?

T. rex

caveman

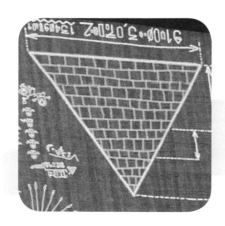

pyramids

banana

See these funny yellow creatures?

They are called Minions.

Minions are small and round.

They go by many names,

like Dave, Paul, Carl and Mike.

Each Minion is different,
but they all share the same goal:
to serve the most despicable master
they can find.

Minions have wandered the earth
for millions of years,
searching for the perfect villain
to be their master.

Masters were not hard to find,
but they were hard to keep.
Something always went wrong.

First there was the T. rex.
The Minions followed
the mighty beast as he stomped
through the forest.
They scratched his back.
They scrubbed his head.

They sent him flying
into a volcano by mistake.
"Whoops!" said the Minions.

Next came the caveman.
The Minions helped him
fight off wild animals.

Well, most of the time.

Minions have served some of the greatest leaders in history.
Or they have tried to, at least.

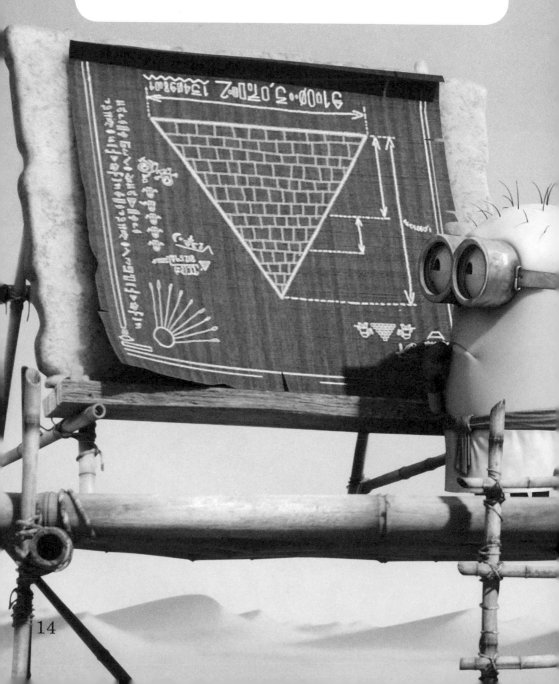

They built the pyramids in Egypt, but they built them upside down. This caused the pyramids to fall . . . right on top of the pharaoh.

Then the Minions made Dracula
their master, until they accidentally
turned him into stone.

The Minions moved
from one evil villain to another.
They never seemed to find
their perfect fit.

Once, they stood by one of the world's
fiercest and shortest generals.
It turned out that Minions
do not make very good soldiers.

The Minions did not give up hope,
no matter how often they failed.
And they failed a lot.

Finally, after being chased away
by the little general's army,
the Minions built a new home.
It was big enough for the whole tribe.

The Minions were safe.

They were secure.

They had everything

they could ever need.

But still, something was not right.
Without a bad guy to serve,
they had no purpose.

They became sad and aimless.
The Minions did not know
what to do.

But all was not lost,
for one Minion had a plan.
His name was Kevin.

Kevin would leave the cave
and not return until he found
his tribe the biggest, baddest
villain to serve!
But he needed help.
"Buddies," said Kevin.
"Kiday come me!"

"Me coming!" said Bob,
the littlest Minion.
He was ready to help.
From the back of the room,
another hand went up.

Stuart had been volunteered by his friends while he was napping. And so the three Minion heroes got ready for their journey.

Kevin felt pride.

He would be the one to save his tribe.

Stuart felt hungry.

He would be the one to eat this banana.

And Bob?

Bob was scared of the journey ahead.

But as long as they stuck together,

Bob knew everything would be okay.

"Let's go!" cried the three
Minion friends.
It was time to find
a new despicable master!